"I **wish** I was a superhero flying through the air.
I'd battle all the baddies in my bright red underwear!"

"A superhero's never scared –
they're much too **brave** and **bold**.
If being brave became a sport,
they'd always win the **gold**."

SUPERHEROES DON'T GET SCARED

... OR DO THEY?

Maisie Brown was
feeling scared,
and oh so very small.

"It's just not fair,"
she cried out loud,
"I don't feel brave at all!"

But Maisie frowned and shook her head.
"That *can't* be true at all!
Burpnado flies around to look
for trouble, big and small."

"From jiggly-wiggly jellyfish
to **wobbly jelly** treats,
they make her want to run away
and **hide** beneath her sheets."

"I bet Specstacular," said Maisie,
"never feels afraid.
When anyone's in danger,
she comes **dashing** to their aid!"

"She spots the baddies from afar,
and sets her specs to MAX.
Then, ZAP! Out shoots a Super Ray,
which stops them in their tracks!"

ZAP!

"In fact ..."

said Mum,

"... there is one thing
that takes away her spark.
Specstacular is terrified
of being in the ...'"

"She panics when she cannot see.
It makes her want to sob.
She always takes Night-Vision Specs
to each and every job."

"Alright," said Maisie with a frown,
"but BogeyBoy's bravetastic!
His bogey blasts are sticky, strong
and ever so elastic!"

"From slimy slugs to wiggly worms
and even *teeny* ants,
they scare poor BogeyBoy so much,
he **jumps** out of his pants!"

"Okay," said Maisie slowly,
"but when Jelly Blob attacked,
Burpnado burped him up to space!
I know that for a FACT!"

"And after Blackout Burglar Bat
switched off the moon and sun,
Specstacular raced through the dark,
not stopping 'til she won!"

"And just last week, when Disco Bug
forced everyone to dance,
brave BogeyBoy launched bogey balls
that stopped the bugs mid-prance!"

Maisie smiled and crossed her arms,
"You see, you are quite wrong.
No superhero's *ever* scared.
They are too brave and strong."

Dad shuffled close to Maisie and
then whispered in her ear,
"But bravery cannot exist
unless you first feel …

"To feel afraid is normal, and it happens to us all.
Your tummy flutters, flips and flops.
It makes you feel so small.
But when you choose to face your fear,
whatever it may be,
then something magic happens ..."

"You may not battle baddies, or bring crime down to zero,
but you would still be just as brave as any superhero."

Maisie smiled. She still felt scared, but that was now okay.

"Just call me SUPER MAISIE! I am feeling brave today!"

For Oliver and Harry — my own, very special, superheroes.
For Nicholas, who helped me to be brave enough to write my stories.
And for all the little superheroes who face their own fears every single day – K.T.

For every mum out there – you are the biggest superheroes I know – C.E.

UPS!DE DOWN BOOKS

First published in Great Britain in 2020 by Upside Down Books, an imprint of Trigger Publishing

Trigger Publishing is a trading style of Shaw Callaghan Ltd & Shaw Callaghan 23 USA, INC.
The Foundation Centre
Navigation House, 48 Millgate, Newark
Nottinghamshire NG24 4TS UK
www.triggerpublishing.com

British Library Cataloguing in Publication Data

A CIP catalogue record for this book is available upon request
from the British Library

Paperback ISBN: 978-1-78956-163-0

Kate Thompson and Clare Elsom have asserted their rights under the Copyright,
Design and Patents Act 1988 to be identified as the author and illustrator of this work.

Design by Kathryn Davies
Printed in China
Paper from responsible sources

Helping children understand their emotions as well as identifying the same feelings in other people is an important step in their emotional wellbeing and positive mental health. *Superheroes Don't Get Scared is* a brilliant and insightful book, which normalises the experience of fear and anxiety, as well as encouraging children to face their fears and find their inner (super) powers.

It's a very humorous book, and children will love the fun characters and their exciting adventures. Perhaps most importantly, they will also be able to relate to Maisie and the message at its heart: that fear is felt by even the bravest hero… and that's okay, because to recognise fear is the first step in facing it. Everyone will enjoy reading this story – parents, children and superheroes alike!

Lauren Callaghan

Consultant Clinical Psychologist,
Co-founder and Clinical Director of Trigger Publishing